First Hardcover Edition, November 2015 10 9 8 7 6 5 4 3 2 1

ISBN 978-1-4847-1551-2
FAC-03427-15261
Library of Congress Control Number: 2015944690

Printed in the United States of America

For more Disney Press fun, visit www.disneybooks.com

THE
LION
GUARD

RETURN OF THE ROAR

BASED ON THE LION GUARD SERIES DEVELOPED
FOR TELEVISION BY **FORD RILEY**
ADAPTED BY **VICTORIA SAXON**
ILLUSTRATED BY **MIKE WALL**

𝒟𝒾𝓈𝓃𝑒𝓎 PRESS
Los Angeles • New York

As the sun rises over the African savannah, Simba sits next to his daughter, Kiara, atop Pride Rock.

"Everything the light touches is part of our kingdom," Simba says.

"HEADS UP!" someone shouts. "INCOMING!" It is Simba's son, Kion. He and his friend Bunga are playing a wild game of Baobab Ball.

"Kion," Simba says, "I'm talking to your sister about something important."

"Because," Kiara continues, "I'm training to be—"

"Queen of the Pride Lands," Kion finishes. "Yeah, yeah, I know all about it."

"ZUKA ZAMA, KION!"

Bunga sings out as he jumps off Pride Rock.

"Game on, Bunga!" Kion shouts back.

The two best friends chase each other around the Pride Lands.

They hop on hippos' heads, startle a snake, and wrestle each other until . . . the baobab fruit lands in the Outlands.

"Game over," Kion calls to Bunga. He knows there are dangerous hyenas nearby.

"I'm not afraid!" Bunga exclaims as he heads down into the Outlands.

Suddenly, Janja the hyena spots Bunga. "Now that's my idea of a delicious lunch!" Janja growls. "Chungu! Cheezi!" he calls to his pals. "Bring that honey badger to me!"

"Let him go!" Kion shouts.

But the hyenas just laugh at him.

"I said, let him go!" Then Kion roars!

R-R-R

Bunga escapes from the stunned hyenas and scampers up the ridge to Kion.

"How did you do that?" Bunga asks.

"I don't know," Kion replies. "It just happened."

"Well, it was UN-BUNGA-LIEVABLE!"

Bunga laughs.

Kion's roar echoes throughout the Pride Lands, all the way to Pride Rock.

"Do you think that was Kion?" Simba asks Rafiki. "He can't possibly be ready. He's still a cub."

At that moment, Kion arrives with Bunga.

"We have heard your roar!" Rafiki says excitedly. Rafiki explains that Kion has the Roar of the Elders. "The great lions of the past roared with you. Now it is time for **YOU** to lead the Lion Guard."

Simba and Rafiki lead Kion and Bunga to a secret meeting place.

"The Lion Guard is the team that protects the Pride Lands and defends the Circle of Life," Simba explains. "And this is where they used to meet."

"Your great-uncle Scar also had the gift of the Roar," Simba continues. "He wanted to get rid of his brother, Mufasa, so he could be king. But the Lion Guard refused to help Scar, so he used the Roar to destroy them. By using the Roar for evil, Scar lost its power forever."

"Starting today, you are the leader of the new Lion Guard!" Simba tells his son.

"The gift of the Roar makes you the **FIERCEST** animal in the Pride Lands. I need you to assemble a team of the

BRAVEST,

FASTEST,

STRONGEST,

and

KEENEST OF SIGHT."

Kion gets started right away. "You're the bravest animal I know!" he tells Bunga. "I want you to join the new Lion Guard."

"ZUKA ZAMA!"

Bunga exclaims. He is so excited that he goes to tell his uncles, Timon and Pumbaa.

But Pumbaa is concerned. "It sounds like it might be dangerous."

"It's worse than that," adds Timon. "It sounds like work!"

Finally, Bunga wins them over. "Congratulations, Bunga!" Timon cries.

Mzingo the vulture
overhears the news about the
new Lion Guard and flies to the
Outlands to tell the hyenas. Janja
and Mzingo form a plan to attack all
the animals they can before the new Lion
Guard is in place.

"Tonight we strike!" the hyenas chant.

Meanwhile, Kion knows exactly where to find the rest of his Lion Guard.

FULI
the cheetah
is the fastest.

BESHTE
the hippo
is the
strongest.

ONO
the egret
is the keenest
of sight.

Kion gathers his friends to explain what the Lion Guard is.

"So who's the fiercest, Kion?" Fuli wants to know.

"Show them the Roar!" says Bunga.

Kion hesitates. He doesn't want to abuse the power of the Roar and end up like Scar. Still, he can't help showing them the Roar just once.

"Okay," he says, "this is the Roar!" Kion steps back and takes a deep breath.

But the only sound he makes is a tiny squeak!

Just then, Simba arrives, ready to meet the new Lion Guard.

"Kion, the Lion Guard has always been made up of lions," Simba scolds. "This isn't a game for you to play with your friends."

Needing to be alone, Kion wanders out into the Pride Lands.

"Kion." A voice comes from the clouds. It is Mufasa, one of the great kings of the past.

"Grandfather!" exclaims Kion.

Kion confesses his fears to Mufasa. "Maybe I'm not ready to lead the Lion Guard or to use the Roar." He sighs. "I don't want to end up like Scar."

"Trust yourself, Kion," Mufasa advises.
"The Roar will be there for you when you need it.
And so will I . . . until the Pride Lands' end."

As Mufasa's face fades from the sky,
Kion hears Bunga calling to him.

"The hyenas!" Bunga exclaims.
"They're attacking the gazelles!"

Kion and Bunga race off to find
the rest of the Lion Guard.

"Let's go!" Kion calls to his team.

Before they head out, Kion places his paw on each of his friends' shoulders to give them the mark of the Lion Guard.

The Lion Guard quietly creeps down to the gazelles' grazing area.

Suddenly, Kion stands up and takes the lead.

"TILL THE PRIDE LANDS' END, LION GUARD DEFEND!"
he shouts.

"COMING THROUGH!"
Beshte yells.

**"NOWHERE TO RUN THAT
I CAN'T RUN FASTER!"**
Fuli shouts.

"LOOKING FOR SOMETHING, FEATHERNECK?"
Ono says to Mzingo.

"ZUKA ZAMA!"
Bunga calls.

R-R-R

"Well, if it isn't Kion the lion cub!" Janja sneers.

"We're the Lion Guard, Janja," Kion replies.
"We defend the Circle of Life. You and your kind
are not welcome in the Pride Lands. Ever!"

Kion takes a deep breath and lets out
a roar so powerful that it sends the
hyenas running and stumbling back
into the Outlands.

Simba watches everything from a nearby ridge. He could not be prouder of his son.

"I told you, Simba, he is ready!" Rafiki shouts. "It is time!"

"Yes," Simba agrees. "It is time. Time for the Lion Guard!"

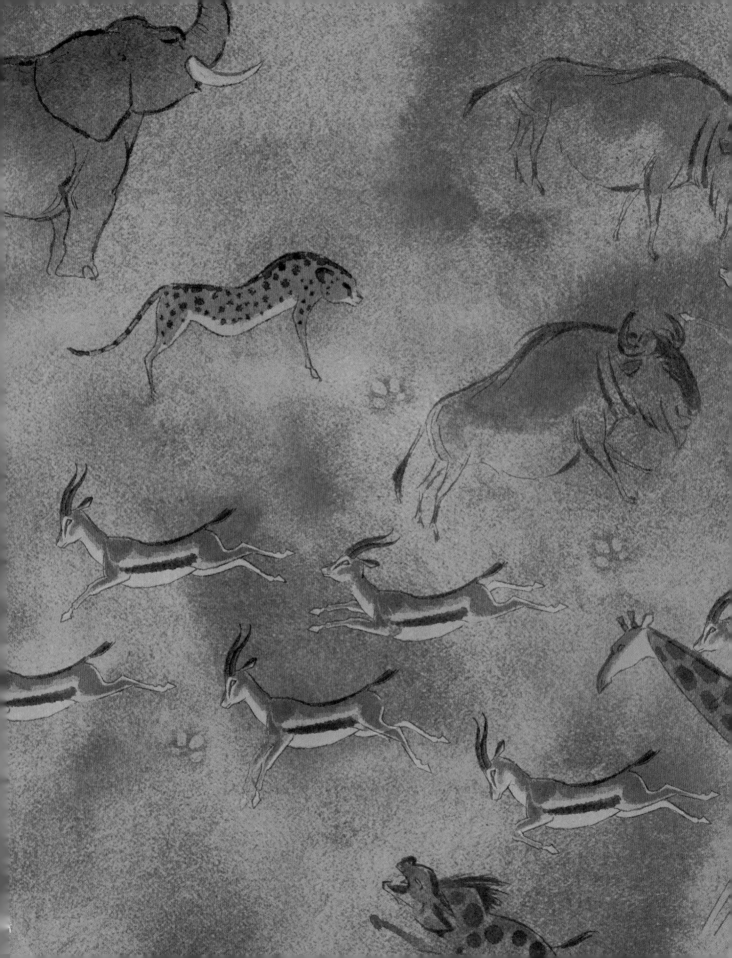